W9-BJM-419

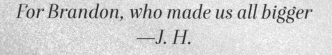

For Brandon, who made us all bigger
—J. H.

For my grandma Loah, who encouraged me
to be fabulous at every opportunity
—L. H.

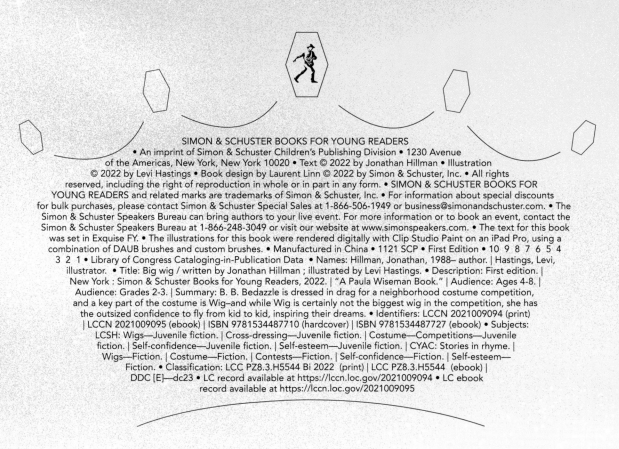

SIMON & SCHUSTER BOOKS FOR YOUNG READERS
• An imprint of Simon & Schuster Children's Publishing Division • 1230 Avenue
of the Americas, New York, New York 10020 • Text © 2022 by Jonathan Hillman • Illustration
© 2022 by Levi Hastings • Book design by Laurent Linn © 2022 by Simon & Schuster, Inc. • All rights
reserved, including the right of reproduction in whole or in part in any form. • SIMON & SCHUSTER BOOKS FOR
YOUNG READERS and related marks are trademarks of Simon & Schuster, Inc. • For information about special discounts
for bulk purchases, please contact Simon & Schuster Special Sales at 1-866-506-1949 or business@simonandschuster.com. • The
Simon & Schuster Speakers Bureau can bring authors to your live event. For more information or to book an event, contact the
Simon & Schuster Speakers Bureau at 1-866-248-3049 or visit our website at www.simonspeakers.com. • The text for this book
was set in Exquise FY. • The illustrations for this book were rendered digitally with Clip Studio Paint on an iPad Pro, using a
combination of DAUB brushes and custom brushes. • Manufactured in China • 1121 SCP • First Edition • 10 9 8 7 6 5 4
3 2 1 • Library of Congress Cataloging-in-Publication Data • Names: Hillman, Jonathan, 1988– author. | Hastings, Levi,
illustrator. • Title: Big wig / written by Jonathan Hillman ; illustrated by Levi Hastings. • Description: First edition. |
New York : Simon & Schuster Books for Young Readers, 2022. | "A Paula Wiseman Book." | Audience: Ages 4-8. |
Audience: Grades 2-3. | Summary: B. B. Bedazzle is dressed in drag for a neighborhood costume competition,
and a key part of the costume is Wig—and while Wig is certainly not the biggest wig in the competition, she has
the outsized confidence to fly from kid to kid, inspiring their dreams. • Identifiers: LCCN 2021009094 (print)
| LCCN 2021009095 (ebook) | ISBN 9781534487710 (hardcover) | ISBN 9781534487727 (ebook) • Subjects:
LCSH: Wigs—Juvenile fiction. | Cross-dressing—Juvenile fiction. | Costume—Competitions—Juvenile
fiction. | Self-confidence—Juvenile fiction. | Self-esteem—Juvenile fiction. | CYAC: Stories in rhyme. |
Wigs—Fiction. | Costume—Fiction. | Contests—Fiction. | Self-confidence—Fiction. | Self-esteem—
Fiction. • Classification: LCC PZ8.3.H5544 Bi 2022 (print) | LCC PZ8.3.H5544 (ebook) |
DDC [E]—dc23 • LC record available at https://lccn.loc.gov/2021009094 • LC ebook
record available at https://lccn.loc.gov/2021009095

BIG WIG

WRITTEN BY
JONATHAN HILLMAN

ILLUSTRATED BY
LEVI HASTINGS

A PAULA WISEMAN BOOK

SIMON & SCHUSTER BOOKS FOR YOUNG READERS

NEW YORK   LONDON   TORONTO   SYDNEY   NEW DELHI

This is Wig.

Wig belongs to
B. B. Bedazzle,

the most fabulous
queen, by far.

When B. B. takes
the stage . . .

Wig **grows** when
the lights *snap*.

Wig **grows** when
the people *clap*.

BIG
WIG
BALL

When the music *twirls* and *tangles*,

Wig forgets one tiny fact.

STAGE

Wig is
not
very
big.

These are the **big** wigs.

T E E T E R I N G

T O W E R I N G

atop the
other
queens.

They're all here for the BIG WIG BALL!

The only night when Wig feels small.

WHOOOSH

This is Wig,
wigging
out.

Nowhere to hide,
Wig hitches a ride

ARF!

on the head of
this little guy.

But with Wig on his side . . .

little is a little
less
little.

He stands a little taller.
He puffs out his chest.

He believes that **he** is the **best**.

And the bigger *he* believes,
the bigger *Wig* believes too.

Wig remembers what wigs can do.

Wig brushes the world **bolder**, brighter hues.

BOING

Wig hears whispered wishes . . .

and turns them into
something true.

The bigger their dreams,
the bigger Wig seems.

Everyone wants
Wig on their team!

One by one,
Wig gives them a try.

And all together,
they help Wig fly!

HIGHER, HIGHER

HIGHER

above Wig's fear.
All the way up, where
Wig can see clear.

B. B. Bedazzle needs
Wig most of all.
Without her Wig . . .
B. B. IS
BALD!

Wig **frizzes** and **fizzles**
and splits her ends,

flying home FAST
to find her friend.

SWOOSH

Wig makes B. B. bigger.

BIGGER
when the lights snap.

BIGGER
when the people clap.

BIGGER
when the music
flips and *flows*.

That's how
Wig knows . . .

WIG IS BIG ENOUGH
to **win** the prize.

Big enough
no matter her size.